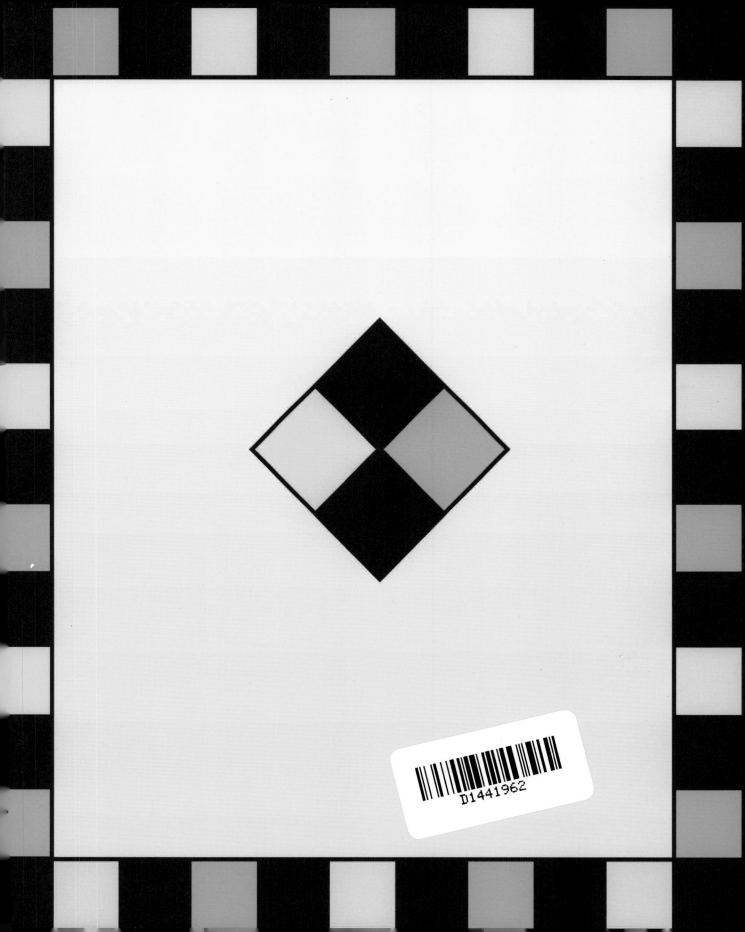

Divorce Stinks!

Divorce Stinks! by Paul M. Kramer

© Paul M. Kramer October 2014. All Rights Reserved.

Aloha Publishers LLC
848 North Rainbow Boulevard, #4738
Las Vegas, NV 89107
www.alohapublishers.com

Inquiries, comments or further information are available at, www. alohapublishers.com.

Illustrations by BJ Nartker, bjnartker@gmail.com
Audio by Charly Espina Takahama charly@pmghawaii.com
Collaborator, Co-Editor, Cynthia Kress Kramer

I would like to dedicate this book to Dr. Ernest Bordini, owner of Psychology Associates of North Florida. drejb@cpancf.com Dr. Bordine has not only been a friend, his insight, feedback and suggestions have ultimately been instrumental in raising the quality level of my writing. I appreciate the friendship and the collaboration.

ISBN 13 (EAN): 978-0-9819745-4-5
Library of Congress Control Number (LCCN): 2009902668
Printed in Guangzhou, China. Production date: September 2014 Cohort: Batch 1

Divorce Stinks!

by Paul M. Kramer

Aloha
PUBLISHERS
Books & Stories by Paul M. Kramer

My mother told me it wasn't my fault that my father moved away.

She said I wouldn't understand now, but I would some day.

Do you think if my parents loved me more they wouldn't have done this to me?

I really love my daddy and my mommy both equally.

I'm not sure that they understand how badly this is affecting me.

I wish everything could go back to the way it used to be.

It feels like my whole world has been turned inside out.

I no longer feel safe and comfortable and I'm filled with doubt.

Why did they have to break-up and tear my family apart?

The thought of my daddy living somewhere else hurts my heart.

Sometimes I wonder if I am not the child they hoped I would be.

I'm not sure that they care enough, even though they say they love me.

"My name is Kate, I'm 9 years old, and I am in the third grade.

Before my parents divorced, I do not remember ever being afraid.

I really need a friend who can understand what I'm going through.

Maybe just maybe that special new friend could be you."

I wanted to talk to someone who had similar problems as I now do.

My friends' parents who are not divorced have never gone through what I am going through.

Do you think, if I tell my friends and my teacher, they will think any less of me?

Especially now, that I come from a broken family.

My mom told me about something she read on the internet.

She was going to buy me a puppy so I could have a pet.

It would be good for me, she said, to have somebody else to take care of.

She also said it would not replace my daddy, but it would be someone else that I could love.

My mother doesn't understand that buying me things will not make everything all better.

But at least she's trying, so as far as buying me the dog, I let her.

"Don't worry," she said, "in time everything will be alright."

My mom tucked me in, gave me a hug and a kiss and said, "Good night."

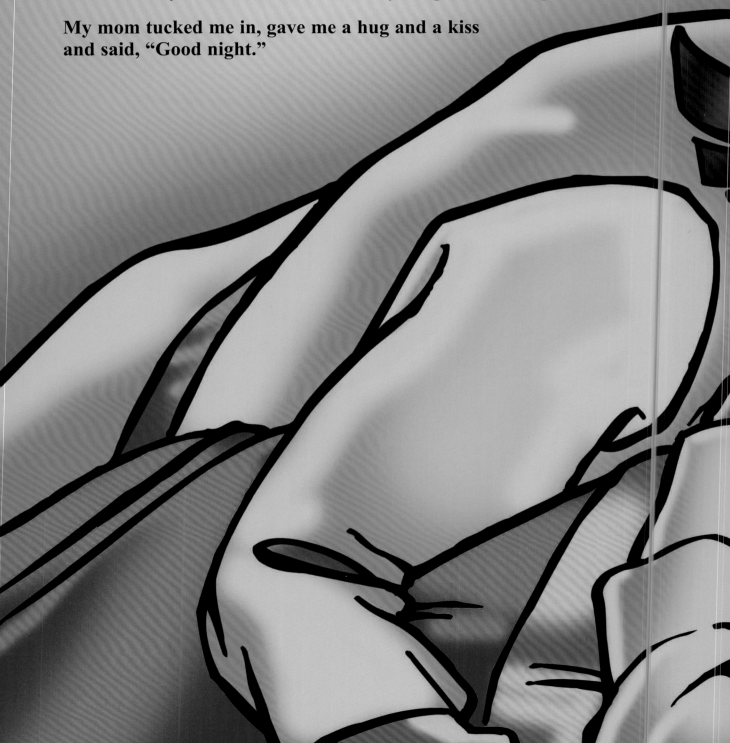

The next weekend, my dad picked me up and showed me where he was going to live.

I had difficulty remaining calm and staying positive.

He said he was so sorry for the way things worked out and wished there was a better way.

He tried his very best to show me that he loves me the entire day.

Millions of couples get divorced every year.

Children often suffer the most, which really isn't fair.

Parents are painfully aware that their choices and decisions will affect you.

Kids cannot be blamed for what their parents decide to do.

When parents finally decide to separate or get a divorce, there isn't too much their children can do.

It may be hard to see now but your parents will do everything possible to continue to support and protect you.

Too often things do not work out the way parents hope and want them to.

But most importantly, it does not mean that they do not truly love you.

It is good to trust your family and friends regarding how the separation or divorce is affecting you.

You can share your feelings and tell them if you're scared and worried or unsure of what to do.

Nothing can ever change that special spirit that lives inside your heart.

Your parents gave you the gift of life despite that they're now apart.

It is very important to talk about your feelings and to say what's on your mind.

Don't be embarrassed to talk about anything troubling you, most everyone will be understanding and kind.

Always remember, your mother and father have divorced each other, they have not divorced you.

Instead of having one family home to live in, you might now have two.

Divorce stinks and can cause many unwanted new fears.

It generally brings with it much sadness and lots of tears.

You are worthwhile, you deserve to be happy and it's
alright to cry.

You and your parents will somehow get through this
if you all try.

So please believe that you are not at fault for your parents' separation or divorce or for anything else they do.

Adults make mistakes, but they didn't make a mistake about having you.

You do not have to be a victim; the rest of your dreams can come true.

Divorce does stink, and when you get older and someday get married, it doesn't have to happen to you.

Other Books Available by Paul M. Kramer

This story was written with the intent to motivate children to seek help when being bullied. Bullying is a very serious problem that has reached unacceptable and uncontrollable levels in recent years and must be dealt with.

Mikey was unwilling to be bullied any longer. Although Mikey was taking karate lessons to learn self-defense, he realized that fighting the bullies was not the best way to solve his problem. Instead, he found the courage to tell his teacher, which turned out to be the right thing to do and as a result the bullies were held accountable for their actions.

This is a must read for children and for the parents of young children who are having problems with bullies and bullying.

ISBN: 978-1-941095-14-0, retail price: $15.95, size: 8" x 10"

Other Books Available by Paul M. Kramer

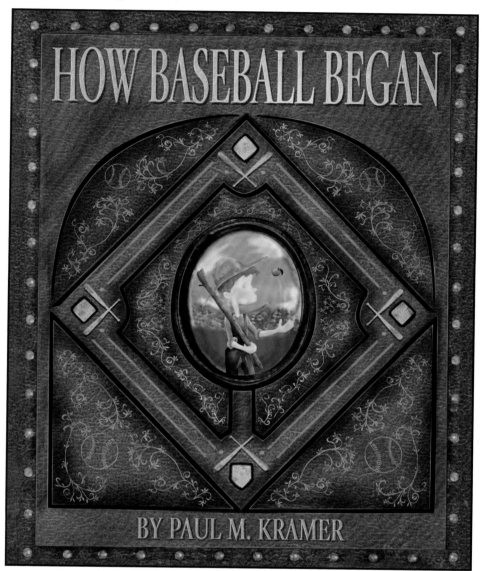

How Baseball Began – How did America's beloved game of baseball actually begin? This informative sweet story written in rhyme tells us. It educates newcomers about the fundamentals of the sport and the basic rules of the game. Both big and little leaguers will be entertained and delighted by the logical, step by step progress the story presents, from baseballs simple beginnings to the game we know today. The big question is, did baseball really begin the way Clem, Carl, and Fred said it did?

ISBN 13 (EAN): 978-0-9819745-9-0, retail price: $15.95, size: 8" x 10"

Other Books Available by Paul M. Kramer

"Zeep Needs More Sleep" was written to motivate children to sleep more, to become more focused in school, to be less cranky and to be happier. This charming tale about a town of pigs whose lives were drastically improved when a boy named Philippe who loved to sleep saved his friend Jim's life due to his courage and quick reflexes. The Mayor of the town presented Philippe with a medal and asked everyone in the town to honor Philippe, by going to sleep just one hour earlier each night for just one week. The results were so amazing that after the week had ended just about everybody was happier and nicer to each other and continued to sleep more than they did before.

ISBN: 978-0-9827596-0-8, retail price: $15.95, Size: 8" x 10"

This is a heartwarming story about a 14 year old girl named Maggie who loved to play sports but found it difficult to reach her potential because of her weight issues. She changed her life by altering her eating habits and exercising regularly. As a result she became more physically fit and was able to achieve her goal of being the best she was capable of being. She also realized that nutritious foods could actually be quite tasty. Through time, regular exercise and better eating habits, Maggie's confidence improved and she was healthier and happier.

ISBN: 978-0-9827596-7-7, retail price: $15.95, size: 8" x 10"

About the Author

Paul M. Kramer lives in Hawaii on the beautiful island of Maui with his wife Cindy and their son Lukas. Paul was born and raised in New York City.

Mr. Kramer's books attempt to reduce stress and anxiety and resolve important issues children face in their everyday lives. His books are often written in rhyme. They are entertaining, inspirational, educational and easy to read. One of his goals is to increase the child's sense of self worth.

He has written books on various subjects such as bullying, divorce, sleep deprivation, worrying, shyness, and weight issues.

Mr. Kramer has appeared on "Good Morning America," "The Doctors," "CNN Live" as well as several other Television Shows in the United States and Canada. He's been interviewed and aired on many radio programs including the British Broadcasting System and has had countless articles written about his work in major newspapers and magazines throughout the world.

More information about this book and Paul M. Kramer's other books are available on his website at www.alohapublishers.com.

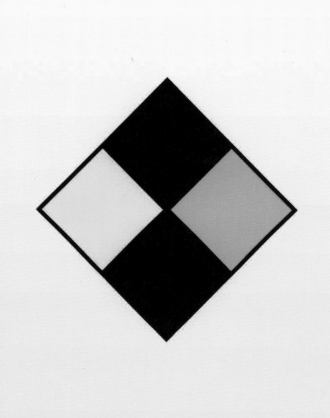